Jordan's Confessions

Charmaine Galloway

Jordan's Confessions

A Short Story

Charmaine Galloway

www.charmainegalloway.com

Charming Gal PUBLICATIONS

ISBN-13: 978-0692475850

ISBN-10: 0692475850

Cover Designer: Dynastys Cover Me

Acknowledgements

I would first like to give thanks to God for blessing me with a talent to write stories that will hopefully inspire, educate, and entertain others.

I would like to thank all the people that have read all of my books and that have encouraged me to keep writing. I would also like to thank *you* if this is your first time reading my work, I appreciate you for giving my work a chance. I hope that you will check out my other books.

Shout out to Racquel Williams and K. K. Burks for keeping me focused on my writing. When I was MIA they would call me and encourage me to get back in the groove of writing. Thanks ladies for pushing me to do what I love to do, write.

Last but not least, I would like to thank my editing team Perfect Tense Editing and Lisa Muhammad thank you ladies for helping me to perfect my craft. I couldn't have done this book without you.

When something bad happens, you have three choices...You can either let it define you, let it destroy you, or you can let it strengthen you.

-Jordan Colbert

Prologue

My thoughts raced and my head felt as if it would explode. The torture that happened to me just seconds ago played over in my mind like a scratched DVD that kept skipping. I sat in the center of my bed, my body locked in the fetal position. I was so confused.

Why? Why had this happened to me? Why me, Lord? I'm not a mean person, I don't go around doing callous things to others. Then thoughts of my friend flashed through my mind.

Wait a minute…

Maybe God was punishing me for what happened to my friend, Heaven.

"I didn't mean to cause her any pain. And I really didn't want to be the reason she…committed suicide," I cried out loud as my heart pumped spastically.

Just the thought of her and what she must have gone through the night before she passed away made my stomach turn. I scooted to the edge of my bed, placed my head in my sweaty palms and cried uncontrollably. I cried for her and I cried because what I had just gone through was almost as bad as what my friend endured. The only difference was that I was still alive.

But I couldn't keep crying.

I had to get myself together before my mom came home and she would be home shortly.

She had never left me alone in the house with him before. But she did this time and now I had to tell her what happened. I had to tell her as soon as she walked through the front door.

No, no… He would be here. A sickening wave of terror welled up from my belly. Once I told, would he deny what happened? Would she believe him over me? I got up and paced my bedroom floor with my arms crossed over my chest. I glanced over at the door knob and my eyes stayed focused there. Chills ran up my spine.

Am I safe? My door had no lock. Would he come in and hurt me again?

"Oh, my God!" I shouted out loud. "I must be dreaming." I slapped myself to see if I would wake up from the horrible nightmare. I felt the sting on my cheek. No, it wasn't a dream, I was already wide awake. And everything had gone horribly wrong.

I thought I was his baby girl. That's what he called me. He'd been so nice to me, then he'd turned on me and did the worst thing anyone could ever do to me.

I shook my head with disgust. He was a grown man, how could this have happened? I trusted him. Maybe he would tell my mom I wanted it to happen. Or that I lead him to do what he did to me. I had seen a lot of shows on TV where teens confessed that something happened that they didn't want to happen and their parents didn't believe them. Then everyone in the family gave the victim dirty stares.

The victim.

Was I the victim?

Was I as much of a victim as Heaven was?

After my friend committed suicide, all I did, day after day, was go to my room and isolate myself from everyone. I carried sorrow in my heart, I had carried so much pain in my soul because I missed my best friend.

And now I had to face *him*.

Him!

Why?

Why did he violate me the way that he did? My brain hurt as I kept going over what took place in my home. I thought he only wanted to talk to me. We always talked. I talked to him about school. About my little brother. I talked to him about what I wanted to be when I grew up, a veterinarian.

He knew that I loved animals. He would go outside with me after dark, to take my dog

Pebbles out because my mom didn't want me outside alone. We played the play station and basketball together outside in the backyard. So how could he turn on me like that?

And could I turn on him the same way?

If I told someone what happened, he would definitely go to jail. Would my mother be okay without him? Would she be able to handle all the bills?

"Oh, no! My brother will have to grow up without a father, just like I did. Will he hurt me even more if he found out that I told?" I asked myself that question and my voice quavered.

I walked up to my dresser, placed both hands flat on the surface and stared into the mirror. I looked at my reflection through blood shot eyes, looked at the pain and disgust that was all over my face. I had to clean myself up. I had to think about how I would ever look in to his eyes with respect again.

I couldn't respect him after he'd totally disrespected me. He'd completely crossed the line. But I couldn't cross that line. I couldn't break up our family. Maybe I would just keep this secret for life.

Maybe I'd endure the pain alone.

Was the pain I had endured, all my fault?

After all, the man that called me baby girl, the man that was the father of my baby brother, the man that my mom trusted and allowed to live in our home, had just... raped... me!

How would I tell my mother?

How would I tell anyone?

Chapter 1

One month earlier…

My legs shook as I walked through the doors of Amazing Grace Baptist Church. I knew that what I was about to witness would be like nothing that I had ever faced in my fifteen years on this earth. I was about to see my friend lying in a casket.

The church was packed with weeping family members and friends that were close to Heaven. I saw a few of our classmates among the crowd and a few of our teachers that had come out to show their condolences to the family.

I took a moment and scanned all of the beautiful floral arrangements that were placed perfectly on both sides of the casket. I took a few steps up as the line of people in front of me made their way closer to say their last good byes to my dear friend, Heaven Goodlow.

My mom placed her hands on top of my shoulders and whispered in my ear, "Are you okay, Jordan? Do you want to take a seat and go up to view her body later?"

View her body? I was about to view the body of my fifteen year old friend for the very last time.

I swallowed the lump in my throat, "No, Mom. I want to go now."

"Okay," she said and we started our walk forward.

As we got closer, my knees got weaker. My mom took my hand and held it tight. I was so grateful for her support.

"Sweetie, I'm right here," she said, trying to comfort me as we walked up to the casket together.

Once there, a few feet away from my friend, the pain was unbearable. All I could do was stare at her face. It looked as if she was sleeping peacefully. Her hair was in medium sized Shirley Temple curls that rested on her shoulders. She wore a short sleeved white dress with pearls laced around her neck and long white gloves that went up past her elbows. She looked like the perfect little angel.

As I stared at her, all I could think of was how bad Tera and Latoya had treated her, how they had set her and me up just so that they could have a big laugh. Those two were bullies that loved to torment others. I despised them as I remembered the last time I saw Heaven alive, like it was yesterday.

"Jordan, is it true?" Heaven yelled out to me in anger as she walked closer to me in the hallway of our high school. "Was I just a dare?" I was speechless at what I had just walked into. She continued with venom in her eyes. "Did Tera and Latoya really dare you to kiss me so that they could go and tell everyone that I was a lesbian?" She was full of rage, I had never seen her that way before.

I swallowed hard. I knew that what I was about to say would hurt Heaven even more than she already was. "I kissed you because they dared me to, but I'm sorry and I didn't mean to hurt you or lead you on in the process. It was just a stupid little kiss. I like you as a friend, Heaven." I exhaled because I was able to get all my words out, but by the look on Heaven's face, I wished I wouldn't have said those words. It looked as if she was going to pass out.

"I cannot believe this is happing to me!" Heaven cried out. "You were never my friend, you were just using me. You would do anything those fools told you to do," she said as she glared over at Tera and Latoya. "That's why you weren't here to have my back when those clowns humiliated me in

front of the entire school," Heaven spoke with bitter resentment.

Then she charged towards me, trying to attack, but Mr. Jacobs grabbed her arm. That's when she spit in my face. At that point Mr. Jacobs was furious and he lifted her from her feet and carried her to the main office. I was speechless as I wiped the spit from my face with the back of my hand. I had deserved that. I was wrong. I did her wrong and I regretted it.

I tried calling Heaven's phone that day to tell her that I was sorry, but her phone was turned off. The next day I found out from the people that witnessed what happened, that Tera and Latoya tormented Heaven in the cafeteria during lunch time. They called her horrible names and nit-picked with her in front of everyone.

They told me that Tera and Latoya, the two evil sisters, took a picture of Heaven and me kissing and posted the picture all over social media. When Heaven got home, her parents, who were the Pastor and First Lady of Amazing Grace Baptist Church, disowned her because no daughter of theirs would be a lesbian. They were even more upset after finding out that Heaven would be expelled from the Christian school because of her irrational behavior.

A few weeks after that incident, Heaven's mother found her unconscious. She was unable to resuscitate her. Her autopsy revealed that Heaven had overdosed on several different types of pain killers.

The hymn that belted from the choir brought me back to reality. My mom and I were still standing in front of Heaven's casket.

"Come on, sweetie, let's take our seats."

I wiped the tears from my eyes with the Kleenex that the church nurse had given me to clear my vision so that I could make it to the pew. When I sat down, I looked up and saw Tera and Latoya staring dead at me from the side of the room. My heart thumped against my chest with anger.

Why are they here? Haven't they done enough? We would not be here saying our last good-bye to Heaven if they hadn't pulled that stunt.

Yes, I had agreed to the dare to kiss Heaven, but I had no clue that they had planned to take pictures and leak them to all of the social media sites. And I bet that was the reason why she took all those pills. She probably thought that would numb her pain. But I don't think she wanted to die. At least I hope not.

I tried to hold back my tears, but I just couldn't control them. My face grew hot with anger, I wanted badly to charge over to them and strangle them both for what they had done. But then, more civilized thoughts overrode my anger. Besides, I knew that anger and rage wouldn't change anything and I was not going to show any disrespect at my friend's home going.

Tera and Latoya would get what was coming to them sooner than later. And I wouldn't worry about it because I knew God didn't like ugly. He would deal with the wrongdoers.

Chapter 2

Even though Heaven and I were only friends for about eight months, I considered her one of my best friends. I remember the day we met, it was the beginning of our sophomore year and we were in math class. I had forgotten my book at home and I noticed that Heaven was watching me as I searched my book bag.

"Hey, would you like to share my book? I see that you can't find yours." She smiled broadly. She had perfect teeth. The first thing I noticed when I talked to someone was their teeth.

"Um, sure… thanks." I smiled back.

"No problem. Your name is Jordan, right?"

I nodded my head with a smile. "Yup."

"Well, my name is Heaven." She said her name with so much passion, like she was a star on Broadway.

"Heaven? That's an unusual name," I said as I fumbled with my pencil. Her name was different. I wasn't trying to throw shade, it wasn't ghetto like some of the names parents gave their children. It was… unique.

"Yeah, I know. My father is a Pastor, he and my mom said that when I was born I reminded them of an angel from Heaven," she said in a joyful voice.

I thought to myself, *Why didn't her parents just name her Angel*? I don't know how, but she must have read my mind.

"When I tell people the story behind my name, most people ask why my parents didn't just name me Angel."

I didn't say anything, I just smirked.

She continued with glee, "They said too many folks named their children Angel and they wanted my name to be special." Then we saw the teacher coming towards us. That's when Heaven scooted her desk closer to mine and placed one side of her book on my desk. I picked up my pencil and pretended I was following the teacher's directions, but heck, neither one of us knew what was going on. After the teacher walked by to make sure we were doing our assignment, we both looked at each other and smiled.

Heaven was always so bubbly, like she didn't have a care in the world. She would help others that were in need and she didn't like to see people hurt. I guess she was like that because she was raised in the church. It seemed like every time I called her she was either going to church or coming home from church. But she really didn't talk much about what went on at service.

She wasn't the type of friend that looked at me differently because I didn't go to church often. And she was not the type of person that would try to throw scriptures at me every chance she got. She was very shy, not too talkative and I could tell that her parents had high expectations for her.

One conversation we had played in my mind.

"Hey, Heaven, what are you doing this weekend?" I asked as we walked home from school.

"Um, I have to go to choir rehearsal on Saturday and of course you know I go to Sunday School and Church on Sunday," she huffed. I could tell that spending so much time at church sometimes overwhelmed her.

"Why you ask?"

"I just wanted to know if you wanted to go bowling or something."

She smiled, "I wish. That would be fun!" Then her smile turned into a frown. "My folks might not let me go. They say the world is full of sin and the only place where I can stay obedient to God's word is at church doing church activities with church folks. They say that'll keep me faithful in His word so that I'll receive all the blessings he has in store for me." She shrugged her shoulders as if to say she just didn't understand.

I thought to myself, How is going bowling not being faithful to God? I didn't ask her to go to the bar and toss back a few bottles of vodka with me. *But I just let it go because I knew that talking about her parents and the things they did and said made her feel uncomfortable at times.*

As the months passed, our friendship grew stronger. But then some people at school started to bring to my attention the fact that Heaven liked me as more than her friend. She liked me as her girlfriend.

I was shocked when they tried to explain to me how Heaven acted different towards me, unlike how she acted towards her other friends. No, I had never seen her socializing with boys, but I just took it that she didn't do that because she knew her parents weren't havin' it.

I saw how she tried to be perfect for the sake of her parents. They had high standards for her and she tried hard to be perfect in their eyes. Heaven never expressed to me that she was bisexual or a lesbian and I looked at her as only a friend. She was a genuine friend to me and that was all that mattered.

I was trying to balance my friendship with Heaven and my friendship with Latoya, but that was proving to be too much. If you were friends with Latoya you had to become friends with her older sister because those two were connected by the hip. They did everything together. Where one was, the other was soon to follow.

I could tell that Heaven really didn't like being around the two girls, so I tried not to bring them up when I was with her.

"Jordan, I'm not trying to say who should or shouldn't be your friends, but them girls aint nothin' but trouble," Heaven spat.

Latoya was the cool sister, but Tera was the evil one. She was older, bossy, and she loved picking on people just to get a laugh out of it. Most of the times Tera did that, Latoya followed right after her older sister like they were playing follow the leader.

"Tera, why do you always follow behind your sister when you know she is wrong?" I wanted to know.

"Girl, you know my sistah is a character, she don't be meanin' no harm. What she does be all out of fun," she giggled. I shook my head because I knew I wasn't going to be able to tell her anything wrong about her sister.

I envied the fact that Latoya and her sister always came to school looking like divas. They wore all the latest name brand clothes, shoes and purses. And their hair was always *on point. I would do anything to be in their shoes for a day, literally.*

I wished that my mom would buy me just a few name brand outfits, I would be so appreciative. I sometimes felt like I didn't fit in. I mean, my mom bought me nice things and I always had what I needed. But she was not going to pay the extra money for a pair of paints or a bag with a label on it.

"Jordan, when you get a job you can buy all the clothes with labels on them that you want. But until then, you are going to wear these nice clothes I bought you with my JC Penny's charge card." That was what my mom always told me.

My mom came into my room and pulled me from my thoughts.

"Hey, Jordan, what are you up to?" She asked as she sat on the edge of my bed.

"Hey, Mom, I was just about to do my homework." I smiled, picked up my book bag off of the floor and unzipped it.

"Did you wash the dishes when you came home from school?" Mom asked

"Yes."

"What! You washed the dishes without me telling you?" She hit me on my leg playfully.

"Yes, Ma." I smiled at her sarcasm.

My mom always worked, but she worked first shift so she would be home when we got out of school. She wanted to make sure that my little brother, Justin, and I had everything we needed.

She was our provider. She provided us with a roof over our heads. She made sure that we had food to eat, clothes on our backs, and that all the bills were paid.

Justin and I had different fathers. My father gave me enough money for school lunch and when I asked for extra money to spend, he would give me a few extra dollars.

When I asked my mom for money, the first thing that came out of her mouth was, "Go ask your dad. You always asking me for money and you see all the things I take care of around the house. Plus, I buy all of your clothes. You can ask yo' dad for anything extra. He should give it to you without asking. He thinks that just because he buys you a lot for your birthday and Christmas that that makes him such a great dad. He makes me sick!" She'd complain.

I'd never seen my mom and dad argue, but my mom would be quick to tell me that my dad made her sick.

My brother's father, Darnell, was a pretty cool guy. He and my mom broke up when she was pregnant with Justin. She said they just couldn't get along. Sometimes I would hear them arguing over the phone, but he was always nice to Justin and me.

Sometimes I would envy the fact that Justin would go and spend the night at his dad's house. I didn't have that privilege as a child. My dad was in and out of jail when I was growing up, but as I got older we got closer. I just didn't spend the night at his house. He had a nice house and everything, but when I went to visit him I sometimes would see spiders and that would totally creep me out.

"Jordan, you can start on your homework, but I will be calling you in a few when dinner is done," my mom said as she stood up and walked out of my room.

"Okay," I said as I started my algebra homework.

I wasn't too excited to eat dinner because she always made the same thing, chicken. And it was either grilled, baked, fried, or smothered. No matter how she cooked it, I was tired of chicken.

Chapter 3

After dinner we took a ride to get some Ice Cream. I loved one dollar scoop Tuesdays at Baskin Robbins. My mom and I would always get Cookies and Cream ice cream and Justin would have to get Chocolate. My brother and I were ten years apart. I was in high school and my brother was in preschool. My mother always said she wanted another child after she got married. Marriage didn't come, but Justin sure did.

"Ma, we getting ice cream?" Justin asked from the backseat.

"We sure are." Mom sang.

"Yes! Ma, I love ice cream!" He shouted cheerfully.

After we drove through the drive-through and ordered our ice cream, we were on our way back home.

"Mom, you know in a few months I can get my temps and then I will have to start practicing on my driving skills," I said, smiling.

"Ugh… I know," my mom said as she smiled and shook her head. Then she continued, "I am not ready for that."

"But I have to learn. You don't want me to get my license then get out on the road and don't know how to drive," I chuckled, but I was dead serious.

"I know, I know, Jordan. I'm going to have to start letting you drive, but I will not be paying for drivers ed. until you get your attitude together and start getting your chores done without me telling you." Her voice was stern.

"Mom, I don't have an attitude and I just did the dishes today without you telling me," I smirked.

"I'm not playing, Jordan," she said seriously.

My mom always thought I had an attitude, but I didn't. Sometimes I just didn't want to be bothered. Sometimes she just nagged, nagged, nagged. She always wanted me to do something. *Jordan, clean your room. Watch your brother. Wash the dishes. Take the garbage out. Geesh, can I get a break!*

"How is school going?" She said, pulling me from my thoughts.

"It's good, I got an A on my math quiz."

"That's great!"

"I got a B on my science test."

"Fantastic! Keep up the good work, sweetie."

I loved school even though I always had a lot of homework to do every night. But it kept my mind stimulated.

"Mom, can I start visiting colleges so I can find out which one I want to go to?"

"Girl, you are staying close to me. You ain't going out of town," she said jokingly.

"I want to go somewhere warm. It gets to cold here in Ohio during the winter."

I guess she was speechless 'cause she didn't say anything. So I continued, "I want to go down south."

"Down South? You don't know anything about down south," she huffed.

Even though she was driving, I turned, looked at her and said, "I know, but I can learn."

"If you are going to go to school out of state, you need to go somewhere where there is family."

"We don't have family out of state," I said in a high pitched but playful tone.

"Exactly, that means you are stuck her with me, forever," she gave me a devilish grin.

"Mom, that grin was creepy." We both laughed out loud.

"You can Google and research a few colleges out of state, but not too far. After you find a few, let me look over them and see if that will be a state that is also fitting for Justin and me," she said with a straight face.

You got to be kidding me!

"You and my lil' brother are not following me when I leave for college," I said slowly to make sure she understood every word that came from my mouth.

"Girl, you cannot, I mean you *will not* tell me where I can or cannot move to." She smiled, but I didn't. I just shook my head and finished eating my ice cream.

I will not be on a college campus with my mom and brother living across the road, I thought. *I don't want to be in the same state as them. I love them and all, but by then I will be a college student and I'll need my own space and privacy.*

Chapter 4

I tried my best not to run into Tera and Latoya in school. I didn't want to be the next person to get expelled for knocking their heads off. But every time I saw them, that moment they lured me into pulling that stunt on Heaven replayed in my mind and I wanted to hurt them.

"Hey, Jordan, where's your little girl friend?" Tera smirked.

I was on my way to gym class. "Why do you always make fun of Heaven, you must want to be her," I said coldly.

"Jordan, don't mind my sister. You know she's just kidding," Latoya piped in.

"Shut up, Latoya," Tera said, giving her sister the eye. "And for you... Jordan, I would never want to be like your lesbo friend," she spat.

"She is not a lesbian. And if she was, why are you bothered by it?" I spat back.

"Yes, she is. Tell me the last time that you saw her even talking to a boy?" She waited for me to answer, but I turned and walked away.

"Hold on, Jordan. I have to ask you something," she said in a friendly tone.

What in the world does she want, I thought. I turned around to hear her out.

"My sistah been telling me that you wished you could afford clothes like ours," she said as she popped the collar on her Coogi button up shirt. Then she waved her Coach purse in front of her to make sure I saw it.

"Whatever. I don't have time for this nonsense," I said in a voice that didn't show her she was telling the truth. I did wish I could afford what they wore, but I was not going to admit that to her.

As I started to walk again she came up and stood in front of me. "Hold up, Jordan. I got some great news for you," she smiled.

What news could she possibly have for me, I thought. "What?"

"I have a few outfits that I was just about to drop off at the Goodwill. I can't fit them and you look like you can so I would rather just give them to you," Tera said, giddy with joy.

Now why was she so darn happy? It seemed like she was up to something. But I couldn't focus on what she was up to because I was thinking hard about how I would look if I came to school with a name brand fit.

I became giddy inside, but I had to ask, "Why are you trying to be nice to me?"

"You are my sister's friend, right?"

Me being your sister's friend has never made you nice to me in the past, I thought. Then I squinted my eyes with confusion and said, "Yes."

"Well, I just want to help out a friend of my sisters," she said, rubbing her hands together. She was acting like I was some sort of a charity case. But I didn't care, I just wanted to get a hold of some of her clothes.

"Girl, you will look dope in those outfits," Latoya added her two cents.

I was geeked up. "Okay... Yes, I want them," I smiled like a kid in a candy store.

"Cool, they are in my car. Come on so I can give them to you."

I looked at my watch. Well I guess I can be late to gym, *I thought.* It will definitely be worth it.

When we made it out to Tera's car, I was shocked that Latoya didn't follow us.

Tera had been telling the truth, though. She had a bag of clothes on the back seat of her brand new Jeep Cherokee. Man, I wished I had the money their parents had. As I looked through the clothes I tried to hold my composure. There were three Coogi outfits and one Prada bag. And they were just my size.

"I love them, thanks so much," I tried to show much appreciation.

"No problem. Girl, you are about to turn some heads when you get in them jeans."

"I know, right," I smiled.

"I have one thing to ask of you and you can be on your merry little way?" Tera said as she shut the car door.

"What?" I asked, caught off guard.

"I dare you to kiss Heaven, just to see if she likes it?" She said in a conniving tone.

What? "Are you out of your mind? I am not kissing no girl. I don't roll like that."

"Girl, calm down. You know that there has been a lot of rumors that Heaven likes you, so you can stop them rumors by just trying to kiss her. If she rejects you then we will know that she is not...you know...a lesbian," Tera said with a devious smile.

Tera was crazy and I was not going to play my friend like that. "Heaven is not gay," I screeched.

"Well, prove it," she barked.

"To who?" I yapped.

"Just to Latoya and me. You and Heaven can meet somewhere and we will be there. Lay one kiss on her lips and see if she rejects you. Then

that will be it. We will put the rumors to rest,"
she said with confidence.

I looked at the bag of clothes and then
back at Tera. I wanted them to stop spreading
rumors about my friend. I'd spent time with
Heaven on a daily bases and I never noticed
her hitting on me. So this dare would be quick
and easy.

It's just a stupid little kiss, I told myself, it
won't hurt anything. I thought about the dare
a little, but my mind was stuck on how I would
look in those clothes.

"You got a deal," I said, agreeing to kiss
my friend on a dare.

Chapter 5

I walked into the living room and my mother was on the phone. She was in shock, I could tell that something terrible had happened. But she always told me to stay out of grown folks business and never ask a grown person questions about stuff that didn't concern me. So I just stayed close and waited for her to get off the phone. The she could 'spill the tea'.

"I just got off the phone with Darnell, his house caught on fire last night," she said in a calm voice.

I figured that he was alright since she was so calm. But I still asked, "Is he okay?"

"Yup, he made it out safe, but the house is not suitable for him to stay in. So he is staying in a hotel for now. I'm just glad Justin was not over there last night."

"What caused the fire?" I was concerned.

"He doesn't know. He said that he was asleep when he heard someone knocking on the door. Then he woke up to the house full of smoke."

"Wow. I'm glad he made it out. I'm glad Justin wasn't there also."

"That was actually Darnell on the phone, he wanted me to drop Justin off so he can spend the weekend with him," my mom said. That was cool that Justin could stay in a hotel. I could remember staying in a hotel a few times when we went out of town for our family reunion. I always liked it "He said that there was a pool there," she continued.

My eyes lit up with joy.

She went on, "He said that if you wanted to go swimming you could."

"Yes, yes! When can we go?" I was anxious.

"We can go now."

"Okay, let me get my swimming suit. Are you going to swim?" I asked

"No, I will just put my feet in. This will be Justin's first time in the pool, but Darnell will get in with him."

When we arrived at the hotel, we met Darnell in his room.

"I see they put you up in a nice spot," my mom said as she entered the room and looked around.

"Yeah, it's pretty decent," Darnell answered.

"Hi, Dad." Justin ran up to his father and hugged him at the knees.

"Hey, Jay," Darnell said as he swooped his son up in his arms.

"Hi," I said shyly and with a smile.

"Baby girl, stop acting shy. Come and give me a hug. I walked over and gave Darnell a one arm hug while he still had Justin in his arms.

"We rode by your house on the way here, it looked pretty bad. Were you able to get anything out of the house?" My mom asked after she sat on the edge of the full sized bed.

She and Darnell were friends. We sometimes did things together as a family, like go out to dinner every once in a while. But most of the time when my mom would drop Justin off, we would go in and stay for a few minutes. I think my mom did that just to see what was going on in Darnell's house.

Sometimes he would have friends over and they would be playing video games or listening to music. My mom and Darnell had broken up when she was pregnant with Justin so sometimes Darnell's girlfriend at the time, would be there. My mom didn't mind.

I would eavesdrop when my mom would be on the phone talking to her best friend Renee. My mom said that she didn't want to be bothered with Darnell's sorry behind 'cause he couldn't keep a job and he had an attitude problem.

He was a good father and she just wanted to make sure that he and Justin had a father and son bond because she didn't want to raise a fatherless son. She said that she would rather be single than be back in a relationship with him. I knew I shouldn't eavesdrop on my mother's conversation, but I did. A lot.

"Nope, I wasn't able to get nothing. The house was full of smoke, all I was trying to do was get out," Darnell said with sorrow in his eyes.

"Man, that's crazy," my mom replied, shaking her head with grief.

"Yes, it is. But, Red Cross came out, they set me up with this hotel and they gave me a voucher so I could get me a few things."

"How long can you stay in the hotel?" Mom asked, trying to get the four-one-one.

"A week. Hopefully by then I will be able to collect the insurance money so I can find me a new place."

The room became silent for a few seconds, Justin was watching cartoons on the TV and I was listening to their conversation. Then Darnell sang, "That's enough about my situation. Are y'all ready to go swimming?"

"Yes." Justin and I blurted out in unison.

"Well, let's go," Darnell spoke and we all got up and made our way to the pool.

The pool room reeked of strong chlorine. The pool itself was huge, it went all the way to ten feet deep. There was also a sauna. Besides us, there was an older couple swimming there. I decided to go and relax in the sauna for a few seconds. Justin wanted to follow me, but I knew he wouldn't be able stand the sauna. It was way too hot for him, but for me it was just right.

Darnell took Justin to the shallow end and carried him on his back as he walked through the water. At first Justin was scared, but then he got used to it and was having a ball. My mom sat on the edge and put her legs in the water.

"Mom, is the water cold?" I asked as I walked towards her.

I had on a black and pink one piece, but my mother always made me wear a swim shirt that was long enough to hang to my thighs. Mom didn't play that, she wouldn't dare let me wear a two piece. Man, in the summer she wouldn't even let me wear shorts. She would say, "Them ain't no shorts, they look like panties."

My shape wasn't all that. I had no boobs, a little booty, and long legs. It wasn't like I had a shape like Beyoncé or somebody, but my mom would always tell me to cover my body and look presentable all the time. She said there were too many crazy folks and perverts in the world.

She would school me all the time about how young girls were coming up missing and ending up in human sex trafficking or lured into prostitution. Sometimes she would talk my ears off about that type of stuff.

"Baby girl, can you swim?" Darnell shouted, pulling me from my thoughts.

"Yes." I answered with a wide smile.

"Well, let's race," he said as he set Justin on the edge of the pool with my mom.

"Y'all can race over there in three feet," Mom pointed with a serious face.

Ugh! "Mom, I can swim in the deep end," I whined. My mom couldn't swim so she was scared of me swimming, sometimes even in three feet of water.

"No, Jordan, ya'll can race over there. Go on, I want to see you beat him," she said in a perky voice as she held on tight to Justin. The boy couldn't breathe because of the fear she had of him falling in.

"Are you ready?" Darnell asked. Both of our backs were against the wall of the pool.

"Yes," I said full of glee. This was going to be fun, I thought to myself.

"Ma, tell us when to go," Darnell shouted. Yes, he called my mother, Ma. He called her that around everybody, even his girlfriend. He even had Justin calling her that, while I called her mom.

"Be careful, Jordan," she added with a stern voice.

Really mom we are in three feet of water. "Okay," I sang

Darnell just looked at her and shook his head.

"Ready. Set." Mom started out.

Then Justin finished when she prompted him to say, "Go!"

We swam to the other end of the pool. I couldn't wait to put my head above water to see if I won.

"Wow, Jordan, you did great!" My mom was excited.

"I won!" I said as Darnell lifted his head up from the water.

"Darn, you beat me," he laughed out loud. He probably let me win on purpose.

Before we exited to pool, Darnell begged my mother to let me go in ten feet of water with him. He stood right by my side as I held onto the edge of the pool and doggie paddled. My mom acted a fool when I let go of the edge and did it alone.

"Jordan, cut it out! Hold on to the edge, you know I can't swim. That's just too much water," she spat as she stood over me, holding on to Justin's hand.

"Ma, she got it. I'm right here. I ain't gonna let her drown," Darnell protested.

I had a ball swimming, I didn't want to leave. While I was swimming, I thought about Heaven. She used to love swimming. She told me she swam like a fish. I would do anything to take just one last swim with my best friend.

I sure did miss her.

Chapter 6

I was getting myself ready for bed and my mom crept into my room.

"Hey, you," she said with a smile.

What in the world was she smiling for at ten at night? "Um, hey," was all I said.

"Are you getting ready for bed?"

That's a pretty dumb question. I looked at my pajamas that were attached to my body and then looked at her. "Yes." I had to think, yes I washed the dishes and I took the garbage out. Something was up, so I wished she just spilled the beans already.

"Well, I want to talk to you about something," she said as she sat on my bed and faced me.

"Okay," I sang. Curious about want she wanted to talk about now, that she couldn't talk to me earlier at the dinner table.

"I just got off of the phone with Darnell. You know he's been staying in that hotel for a few weeks now?"

"Yes," I said, wondering what happened. 'Cause something had to have happened.

"Well, he has to move out this weekend and he hasn't found a place yet. He asked if he could say here for a month or so while he continued to look. So I was making sure it was cool with you.

We are not in a relationship and he will sleep in Justin's room. I just don't want him to be homeless," she explained. She was informing me about this new living arrangement as it I helped pay the mortgage or as if Darnell was a stranger.

Before Justin was born, my mom and Darnell were together. I don't remember how long, but he stayed with us. We had been like a little family, which was when he started calling me baby girl. But that had to be like six years ago, when I was like, nine.

All I could remember from that time was that he loved to cook. I loved to eat his cooking because it was delicious, because he always made different meals that I had never eaten before, and because it wasn't chicken. Oh yeah, and he played basketball with me in the backyard.

"So what do you think?" She asked, breaking me from my thoughts.

"Why you acting like he is a stranger? He is Justin's dad."

"I know. I just wanted to let you know," she smiled and put her arm around me.

My mom wasn't the type of mother that brought men around the house. Darnell had been the only man that had ever stayed in the house with us that I could remember. Once, I had been out to dinner with her friend, Brandon. He was very cool. He would take us to nice restaurants. I wondered what ever happened to him...

"Well, that's what I wanted to talk to you about," she said, breaking me from my thoughts again. She continued, "You get some sleep and I'll see ya' in the morning."

"Goodnight," I said and I pulled my covers up and went right to sleep

Darnell had been staying with us for about a week and it was kind of nice because Justin was out of my hair. They played the Play Station and sometimes I would go in their room and play too. But what I liked most about him staying here was that he cooked something different every day. Most of the time he would ask me what I wanted to eat and he would cook me exactly what I asked for.

We sat at the table and Darnell brought our food to the table. He catered to us. We didn't even have to make our plates, he did. He placed a bowl of what looked like soup in front of me.

"What's this?" I asked.

"It's my special gumbo," he smiled. He knew he was a good cook.

"It smells really good," I said, I couldn't wait to dig in. And when I did, it was delicious.

After we ate, he washed the dishes. He knew I didn't like washing dishes. I really didn't have to do any of my chores once he arrived, 'cause Darnell did them all for me. My mom would get mad and tell him to stop spoiling me because I wouldn't want to ever do anything in life. But he didn't listen to her.

"Jordan, you need to take Pebbles out before it gets dark," my mom said as she put her dishes in the sink.

"I'll go out there with you after I finish washing the dishes," Darnell piped in.

"Okay," I said.

While we were outside, we shot some hoops while Pebbles did her thing.

"I won!" I cheered after I beat him in a game of twenty one.

"Okay, it's getting late. Get the dog so we can go in," he huffed, trying to catch his breath.

I threw the ball in the grass, called for my dog, and started walking towards the gate past Darnell. I don't know what happened, but he then brushed his hand across my butt. I moved out the way and looked in his face with squinted eyes.

"My bad, the gate was in my way."

I was confused about what happened. But all I said was "Okay." And I walked in to the house.

Chapter 7

"Hey, Jordan." I heard a voice say from behind me as I walked from my locker, heading to my science class.

I turned around and Tera was walking towards me. *What could she possibly want with me?* I had been trying to ignore her ever since the funeral about three weeks ago, but I knew that this day would come soon.

I balled up my fist and my face grew hot. I said a quick prayer to myself, Lord please control my anger because right about now I just wanted to go upside this fool's head.

"Why you look so tensed up? I just wanted to say hey. I haven't seen you around. Have you been skipping school?" She grinned.

I was so angry. As I looked in her face, I could see her mouth moving but I didn't hear a word that she said. "What do you want from me?"

"Didn't you just hear me? I said I just wanted to say hey." Tera looked at me, her head titled sideways with confusion on her face.

I took a few steps up to her, I was now close enough to point my finger straight in her face. I talked real slow so she would hear every word I was about to say to her clearly.

"Tera, I would prefer that when you or your sister saw me around you both would look the other way and don't speak to me. Is that understood?" I spoke with bitter resentment.

"Dang, Jordan, why you gotta be so cruel?" She took a step back.

"I don't have nothing else to say to you," I said venomously as I turned and walked away.

"So this is how you act towards me after I generously donated you the clothes off my back," she huffed.

I quickly turned around and began to charge at her. But then I felt a hand grab my arm. It was my friend Teresa.

"Let me go," I growled as I tried to yank away from her hold.

"You do not want to do this. Mr. Scott is watching you and you know he will kick you out of here," she sharply said in my ear.

My heart thumped against my chest, I was furious. I tried to calm myself, but I couldn't. "I ain't no charity case," I said as I eyed Tera critically.

"Girl, bye!" Her words were spoken crudely.

"You killed my friend," I shouted out like a manic.

"Hey, ladies, what's going on here?" Mr. Scott asked with concern in his voice.

"Everything is fine. Jordan's just not feeling good," Teresa said as she put her arm around my neck.

Mr. Scott looked at Teresa and then he observed my tear stained face. "Are you going to be alright, Jordan?"

Teresa looked at me and nodded her head.

"Yes," I whispered.

That was all I could do. I didn't even know I was crying until Teresa wipe my face with a tissue. I had been so angry that it felt like I had just finished ruining a marathon.

I was drained.

Chapter 8

As I walked home alone, I thought about how Teresa came in and stopped me from doing something crazy. The last couple of weeks had been hell for me. I tried to put on a happy face, but inside I was broken. I had never had anyone so close to me die before. It was a hard pill to swallow. I didn't think anyone understood my pain.

I walked up the sidewalk by my house and I saw Darnell planting flowers in the front yard. He must have heard me walk up because he got up from his knees and walked towards me.

"What's the matter baby girl?" He asked with his eyes squinted with concern.

Dang, was it still obvious that I was in pain? "I'm okay, I just had a bad day in school." I tried to cover my sorrow with a smile.

"Well, you don't look okay. Come here," he said in a comforting tone.

I walked towards him and he embraced me like he knew that was what I needed. I laid my head on his chest. I don't know what it was, maybe just the touch of someone comforting me that made me start bawling all over Darnell's shirt. And then the words that came next made me feel a connection with him.

"I understand how you must feel. I had a close friend die too, I was much older than you, but I know that dealing with death can be very hard."

After he said those words I actually felt like someone knew what I was going through. I sniffed and said," How did you get over it?"

He took his arms from around me, pulled my body in front of him and looked me in my eyes. "It will take a while for you get over the loss of your friend. You need to just talk to people that you trust about how you feel. Your mom is here and I'm here when you need me, okay?"

"Okay." I was so tired that I just walked away.

But before I opened the door to enter the house Darnell said. "I know what will make you feel better." I turned around and looked at him. Before I could say anything, he continued. "I can make you some chocolate cookies after dinner. Would you like that?"

He knew I loved chocolate cookies. "Yes," I smiled.

"There's that beautiful smile. But I need you to do something for me."

"What?"

"I need your help baking the cookies," he smiled again.

I smiled back and said, "Okay." Then I walked in the house.

My mom was inside folding laundry. "Hey, Jordan. When you get finished with your homework I'm gonna need you to help me with these clothes?" She demanded without looking up at me.

"Okay." I said as I headed to my room.

Baby girl?" I heard Darnell yelling from the bottom of the stairs.

"Yes?" I answered from my room.

"Dinner is ready."

"Okay," I said as I hoped up from my bed. I smelled the food cooking and I couldn't wait to see what it was because I knew it would be good. I walked into the kitchen and my mouth dripped from shock.

Everything was set up so nicely.

Darnell had done it again, he'd prepared the best meal ever. I loved tacos and he knew it. It was like we had our own little buffet. He cooked different types of meat and placed them in different containers. We could choose from chicken, steak, hamburger and shrimp. He also had the soft tortilla hard tacos shells, all the toppings we needed and Spanish rice served on the side.

We all sat at the table and ate mostly in silence because the food was that darn good.

"I swear you should be a chef," I blurted out after taking a bite of my fourth taco. It was filled with shrimp.

He smiled with gratitude. "Ever since I was young, I loved to cook. My aunt would have me in the kitchen while she cooked, then I started helping her prepare the meals. She gave me all of her recipes. I sure do miss her." He had sorrow in his eyes as if he was thinking of the past with his aunt. She had passed away right before Justin was born.

Darnell cleared our plates from the table. "Are you ready to bake the cookies?" He looked at me cheerfully as if he was a young kid.

"Yes, I am."

"Y'all go ahead and make the cookies while I put Justin in the tub," my mom said.

"Ma, I want some cookies," Justin cried out.

"You can have one when you get out the tub."

Justin pouted and walked out of the kitchen while mom followed behind him.

I got the cookie sheet out of the cabinet and the cookie dough out of the freezer. As we placed the dough on the pan, Darnell asked in a soft tone, "Do you have a boyfriend, baby girl?"

Was this a set up? Was he asking me this question so he could go tell my mom if I said yes? I would be so grounded. "No, I'm too young for a boyfriend," I said with a surly tone.

"Have you ever kissed a boy? You can tell me if you have. It will be our little secret." He gave me a serious look.

"No," I said quickly. Was he asking me because of what my mom found in my phone about a year ago?

"Jordan, come in here right now!" My mom barked. I knew she was upset about something from the tone of her voice.

I timidly walked into the living room where she and Darnell were sitting. He had stopped by to visit Justin.

"What is this?" She held up my cell phone.

Duh! "My phone," I said with confusion on my face. But I knew she must have been looking through my phone.

"I meant what is this in your phone?"

"What are you talking about?"

"You know exactly what I'm talking about. And if you don't start talking, you will be in more trouble!" She roared.

"Uhm, I be on Facebook," I said nervously.

"And?" She wanted to know.

"I talk to boys on Facebook." My heart was beating out of my chest.

"These are not no darn boys, these are grown men," she said matter of factly.

I was silent. I knew they were older because I portrayed myself to be eighteen. I'd never met up with anyone online, I just enjoyed talking to them online. They were more mature than the boys my age, those boys acted like kids.

That night, my mom and Darnell drilled me about how I shouldn't talk to men online. They lectured on and on about how they could be pedophile's or rapist looking for their pray. Even though my mom read all my inboxes and saw that I never talked about sex or told them where I lived, she was still furious with me. Then she deleted my Facebook page and took my phone from me.

"Jordan," Darnell's words brought me back to reality. "I don't mean to pry, but I want to make sure you are not making any wrong decisions. You are like a daughter to me and I want to make sure that you are not letting these big headed boys mistreat you."

"No," was all that came out.

I was a virgin and had never had a boyfriend because my mom would have killed me. I really didn't feel comfortable talking to my mom about boys and I definitely didn't feel comfortable having that conversation with Darnell.

"Dad, did you save me some cookies?" Justin asked loudly as he twirled through the kitchen like the Tasmanian devil. He was right on time, 'cause I was glad to end the conversation that his dad and I were having.

Chapter 9

The sun shined through my window and I knew it had to be close to the time that I would be getting up for school. I was so tired. I had not been able to get a good night's sleep since Heaven committed suicide.

I wondered over and over about whether or not she'd really meant to do that or if it had been an accident. I'd had a dream about how I imagined it was the night of her death. I couldn't see life being that bad, at least not bad enough to commit suicide.

I had seen a lot of people in the entertainment business that had committed suicide. I didn't understand, but I could see how stressed they could be because a lot of people followed their every move and wanted them to act a certain way. They had to live up to other people's expectations and if they didn't, they would be ridiculed and judged by people who really didn't know them.

It was heartbreaking for me to see how Fantasia got through the pain that she endured. People expected so much from her. And she did so much for her family, plus she had to go through the stress that her man was putting her through and the stress of the camera watching her struggles in life. When she took all those pills, I really rooted for her to get better, especially for her daughter's sake.

I loved me some Fantasia and I'd looked up to her ever since she'd won American Idol. That girl could sang. Just thinking about her voice made me go and put her latest CD on and listen to the song that I needed to hear at that moment. Lose To Win.

The first person I saw when I entered into the school building was Teresa.

"Hey, girl, you look cute," she greeted me with a smile.

I waved my hand at her as if I was fanning her off. "Girl, this Aunt Jemima outfit. Quit playing, you know I look a mess." I laughed out loud.

"I was serious. But I'm glad I put a smile on your face."

It did feel good to laugh, but it only lasted a few seconds. Then I was brought back to reality. I still had grief in my heart.

"Hey, Jordan. Why don't you come to camp with me in a couple of weeks? It will be fun. I know you have been through a lot, you know, with the death of Heaven and all. Getting away will probably make you feel a little better," she said hesitantly like she knew I would say no.

"Uhm, I don't know. I will have to see." I really didn't think I was up to going to live in the wild for a week. She had told me that her church took that trip every year. They had church service and did a lot of fun things like swim, have nature walks, and told stories around a camp fire.

"Girl, it will be fun. I need you to come 'cause I need a roommate. I do not want to stay in the cabin with my little sister this year. She snores." We both cracked up laughing.

The school day was long and I was so relieved when the dismissal bell rang so that I could go home and take a nap. My body couldn't take all the sleep I had been lacking.

It was unlike me to miss out on dinner, but today I just wanted to take a nap and eat dinner when I woke up. When I walked in the house, my mom was watching TV with my brother and I didn't see Darnell. I was too tired to ask any questions.

"Hi, mom. I'm going up to my room to take a nap," I told her as I took off my shoes.

"Are you feeling okay?" She asked with concern in her voice.

"Do you have to poop, Jordan?" My brother blurted out. He was a boy and little boys could be so gross.

"I'm okay, mom, I'm just tired. And no, Justin, I don't have to poop." I shook my head and walked up the stairs. After I took my second step my mom yelled out, "You need to stop staying up so late, you wouldn't be so tired."

She didn't know or even care to ask why I was up late. But if she had asked she would have known it was because I *couldn't* sleep.

I don't know how long I was asleep, but my mother came in my room and said that she was going to make a quick run and she would be right back. I just said okay and I was back asleep within seconds.

The kids outside yelling woke me from my deep sleep. I looked at the clock, it was six-twenty-two. I didn't want to get out of the bed because my head was throbbing, but I was hungry so I decided to get up to get dinner and then I would lay back down.

When I went downstairs I was shocked to see Darnell sitting on the couch drinking a beer. I was shocked for a couple of reasons. First of all I thought everyone was gone, second of all I never saw Darnell drinking cause my mom didn't even drink in the house. And third, I was standing in front of him with my tank top and short shorts on that I slept in.

My mom would always tell me not to walk around the house with short shorts on, but that's what I slept in and I thought I was home alone because the house was quiet.

"I'm sorry, I didn't know you were here." I turned around to go back upstairs to put some pants on.

"No, baby girl, you're okay. Go eat your food before it gets colder than it already is. I made you a plate, it's in the microwave," he said as he took a swig from the bottle and then he placed it on the floor.

"Where's my mom and Justin at?" I asked with a whimper. I was exhausted and my head was killing me.

"They went to do something for your grandmother. Do you want me to warm your plate up?" He asked.

He loved catering to us, but I was right in the kitchen. If I wanted my plate warmed all I had the do was push the bottoms on the microwave.

"No, thanks," I said as I quickly gobbled down the tasty meal so I could lie back down.

"Where you going?" Darnell asked in a slurry voice as I walked past him.

"I'm going to lay back down, I have a headache."

"Did you take anything for it?"

"No."

"Come here, I have to tell you something," he said as he scooted to the edge of the black leather couch.

I wondered what he had to say.

"What's that smell?" He asked, sniffing in my direction.

"What smell?" I took a few steps closer to him with confusion on my face.

"What's that you're wearing?" He took both my hands, pulled me slowly and then flung my body to the side of him on the couch.

I was in shock because I knew that what was going on wasn't right. But it was like my feet were stuck in wet cement because I couldn't move them. Then he took my waist and pulled me to the floor. I still didn't move, I couldn't move because my body went numb.

My head pounded so hard that it felt like it would explode. He then put his body on top of mine. What was he going to do? OMG! Suddenly it hit me. He was doing the worst thing imaginable. He couldn't be doing this? Why? Why? Then I felt his hand push my shorts to the side. I inhaled and didn't let the air exhale from my lungs. Then I felt a force of pain as he forced himself inside of me.

Nooooooo!

My mind screamed when my voice wouldn't.

This had to be a dream. But why in the world was I dreaming about something so awful? This was a nightmare that no one would have wished on their worst enemy. My whole body was in pain as he huffed his hot breath in my ear. The moisture from his sweat covered my tank top. He reeked of alcohol.

I had to escape. But I was shocked into sheer immobility. So I used my mind to escape. I wasn't there anymore. I was in the kitchen washing dishes. I was cleaning my room. I was doing homework. I was anywhere and everywhere but there.

I just lay there, I don't know for how long. I heard the kids outside playing, it was still light outside. I wanted to scream out so someone could come save me from this horror. But I was mute. I wanted to call out to my mom so she would come and protect me like she had done in the past when I called her name.

I wanted to stop him, but what if he hurt me even more? What if he hit me? A single tear fell from my eye and I felt it as it rolled down my face to my neck.

Lord, make him stop! My tears clouded my vision. I closed my eyes. Then all of a sudden I got a burst of energy. I felt myself let out a breath, I took the palms of my clammy hands and pushed him off of me with all my might. I didn't say a word as I crawled onto my knees and stood to my feet. I didn't look back as I ran up the stairs to my room and slammed my door close.

There was a monster in my house and I just prayed that my mom would come home soon, before he attacked me again.

Chapter 10

For the past two weeks my life had been a living hell. I had been tip-toeing around the house, not wanting to be seen by my mom or Darnell. How could I tell my mom what went down when she wasn't home? Would she believe me if I told her that her ex-boyfriend raped me?

He raped me.

Every time I thought about what he'd done to me, tears fought to exit my eyes. No matter where I was, no matter how hard I tried to hold them in, I had to release them.

Darnell was no longer sleeping in Justin's bedroom and he'd made it clear to me that he and my mother were officially a couple. During dinner he kissed her on the lips right in front of me. Darnell was not only her boyfriend now, but he would always be Justin's dad.

What if he went to jail after I told? Then Justin would be fatherless, just like I was when I was a child. I not only had to think about how I would be affected by telling, but it would also affect my little brother and my mom. What if they both began to hate me?

My mother seemed to be happy since they were back together. If I told, she would be a single mother again. My mom always complained about not having much money, but now that Darnell was helping her with the bills, would she be angry if he left her after I told the secret that I had been holding on to?

What if he thought I wanted him because I had on those short shorts? What if my mom thought I wore those shorts for him? She had always told me not to flounce around with skimpy clothes on. Did I deserve what he did to me?

My thoughts had been driving me crazy and migraines seemed to be the norm for me. I wished that Heaven wasn't dead. I wished that Darnell wasn't living with us, then we would have never been alone.

It was time for dinner and I really didn't want to join them at the table. As I walked into the kitchen, Darnell had the nerve to try and be nice to me, which really irritated me.

"Hey, Jordan, do you want to make some cookies after dinner?"

You are such a jerk! Was he serious? "No!" I hissed, but I didn't dare look at him.

"Jordan! Why do you have an attitude? He is just trying to be nice. He cooks you your favorite meals and he even washes the dishes for you. What is your problem?" Mom snapped.

Mom he raped me. "I don't have an attitude," I snapped back. I was so irritated

"Yes…you…do! Now apologize," she demanded.

Ugghh. My face twisted in pain. I had no reason to apologize to him. He should have apologized to me. He should have told me that he was sorry for what he had done to me.

I wailed out, "Sorry." And I ran to my room because my tears had won again.

I heard my mom call my name right before she ran after me. But then Darnell followed behind her and I heard him say. "Ma, she must be upset that I'm sleeping in your bed. Give her some time, she'll be okay."

I hated him and I hated what he had done to me. He raped me and now he was sleeping with my mother. At that very moment, I truly thought I knew how Heaven felt the night she took those pills. I just wanted the pain to go away. I wanted the nightmare to be over.

Chapter 11

"Jordan please don't be sad that I'm gone. I'm in a better place. I want you to be happy that I am no longer living in the sinful world. I'm not mad at you. I pray every day that you stay strong and that you don't cry for me."

I jumped up in a panic. My eyes scanned my room as my heart fluttered in my chest. My hair and shirt were damp from my sweat. I had awakened from a dream. I'd seen Heaven, she talked to me. I exhaled and then let out a deep breath. I was glad to know that she wasn't mad at me and that she was in a happy place.

I licked my dry lips. I had to use the bathroom so bad, but I was scared. I was scared because Darnell might be still awake. I never wanted to be around him alone again. I lay back in my bed and I sobbed on my pillow. I wet myself and I sobbed some more.

Another week passed and school was out for the summer. I asked my mom if I could go to camp with Teresa. I really needed to get away, now that I couldn't escape home by going to school. At first my mom was hesitant in allowing me to go to camp because of my attitude, but I thanked God when she said yes. I started to pack. I was ready get out of there.

Thinking back, I remembered how Teresa and I had met our freshmen year…

She and I were not close like Heaven and I, but we talked to each other in passing and in class.

"Do you think you passed that test?" Teresa asked right after our teacher took our completed science tests from her desk.

"I think I did. I like science." I shrugged my shoulders.

"I hate it," she said and we both laughed. "Well, can you tutor me since you are Lil' Einstein?" She smirked.

"Sure," I replied.

My phone rang and it interrupted my thoughts. It was Teresa.

"Hey, girl," I answered.

"Hey, chica. So, are you ready to have fun at camp?" She sounded so energized. I wished I had her energy.

"Yes, I am," I tried to force some excitement into my voice.

"We'll be there to pick you up tomorrow."

"Okay, I'll see you then." We hung up the phone.

The sun gleamed through my blinds as I stretched and lifted my body up. Immediately, I jumped back and leaned against my headboard, my body locked in the fetal position. In less than a heartbeat I quickly grabbed my bedspread and covered my body.

Darnell was standing over my bed. My heart pumped spastically. *Was he watching me sleep? Is he about to harm me again? Where is my mom?* I wanted to ask him those things, but my words wouldn't come out. Perspiration filled my clothes. What did he want?

He just stood there in silence for a few minutes and then he said, "I'm sorry, I didn't mean to hurt you." His face was darkened with pain. Then he turned around and walked out of my room.

I didn't know how to feel. I didn't know what to feel. I was confused. I was lost. I was angry. Was I supposed to accept his apology and go back to living my life like nothing happened? Was he truly sorry? Or did he tell me that so I could keep my mouth closed?

"Uggh!" I screamed out loud as my temples throbbed.

Why was I doing this to myself, allowing my thoughts to drive me crazy? I got up out of my bed and looked at my packed bags that sat beside my door. Today was the day I would escape and be out of that immoral space for a whole week. But my escape would only be temporary because after camp was over, I would have to go back home.

Chapter 12

The ride to the camp resort was about an hour and half. Teresa's parents were really nice. They were amazed at my hair.

"Jordan, your hair is so cute. How did they do that?" Teresa's mom wanted to know as she felt one of my braids.

"This style is called box braids and my mom just added some synthetic hair to my hair and braided it together," I explained.

"The braids are so long. Does it hurt?" Her mom asked. Her face scrunched up as if she was in pain just thinking about it.

"No," I smiled.

Teresa and her parents were Caucasian and they had no clue about how black people did their hair. I was used to the questions. There weren't that many black people in my school, so whenever I went to school with a different hairstyle, or with longer hair than the day before, my teachers would look at me with puzzled looks on their faces and then they would ask me how it was done. Teresa shook her head and gave me a don't-mind-my-mom look.

All the way there we listened to music and Teresa and I played card games in the back seat. When they picked me up, Darnell had the nerve to take my bag and walk it out to the car. I followed silently behind him. My mom and I said our goodbyes in the house, she didn't want to go outside with her head scarf on.

"Wear your seat belt the whole time and keep your phone on so I can call you," she demanded.

"Okay, mom," I answered. She could be so paranoid at times. But I knew she just wanted me to be safe.

After Darnell put my bag in the trunk he said hello to Teresa and her parents then turned to me and said, "We are gonna miss you. Have a good time." Then he hugged me.

Instantly my body stiffened. Smelling his scent turned my stomach. I swallowed the bile that came from my throat. I didn't want him touching me. I wanted to push him away with all my might. But I didn't. I didn't want to cause a scene. I didn't want to do anything to stop me from going on that trip. I didn't hug him back, instead I turned my back to him and got in the car. *Good riddance, you dirty dog*!

"Jordan, we are here." Teresa's voice startled me from my thoughts.

"Great." I smiled as I looked out the window. It looked nice, anything was great at that moment, compared to being at home.

Once I got to the camp, I almost forgot about the incident because I was having a great time. The camp counselors and Pastors of different churches that were there made sure our schedule was full with fun activities. There were about sixteen cabins, designed like small ranch style homes that we slept in. They were big, able to hold eight to ten people.

We had to go to a different building to use the restroom and take our showers. There was a pool that we swam in everyday and there was a park with a basketball court. We went rock climbing, putt-putting, and had tug-of-war in the dirt.

I really didn't think I would have as much fun as I did playing in the dirt. Every morning and night we had church service. Every day we had to paint a poster with the campers in our building, portraying what we learned in the service the night before.

The church services were awesome, the Pastors really did a good job with delivering the word in a way the teens could understand. There was a choir with a guitarist and pianist. After the morning service, I couldn't wait to attend the night service. I wasn't bored like I thought I would be.

In one service the Pastor preached about how to get over the loss of a loved one. I really needed that sermon. He referenced Bible verses when he stated that we all must leave this earth, but we will have eternal life.

We prayed together and they gave us ways to think about the person we lost in a positive manner and not as a sad death or loss. I really received the message and I was able to begin my healing process from losing my friend. Attending the camp was truly a blessing for me.

"Jordan, are you enjoying yourself?" Teresa asked as we sat at the table while eating dinner.

"Yes. I haven't been camping since I was maybe twelve years old when I went with the Boys and Girls Club," I said.

"Really, well I have been coming here since I started high school. So will you come back next year?"

"Yup, I sure will," I smiled.

"This is the last day. Do want to go wall climbing before we have service?"

"Yeah, we can do that," I said as I finished my food.

The choir belted the song, *I Need You Now,* as we entered the building where the church services were held. I heard that song sang before by Smokie Norful.

All the Pastors were lined up in the front of the church. All the camp counselors sat next to their groups. There had to be about one hundred students that were present from different high schools in the area.

After the choir sang a few songs, each of the eight Pastors preached a sermon on a different topic. The last Pastor preached about forgiveness. When Pastor Mathews was preaching, it seemed as if he was speaking directly to me.

He said that we should forgive the people that had hurt us in the past. He said that God forgives everyone so we should too. He also said that if I wanted to live a prosperous life, I needed to repent if I had done wrong, forgive the people that hurt me, and move on. My heart fluttered in my chest as my thoughts raced through my mind.

Should I forgive him? He said he was sorry, but was he really sorry? But why had he done what he did in the first place? Had he violated another girl my age before? He should not get away with hurting people like this. Does God forgive people like him? Does God want me to forgive him?

Silent tears streamed down my face.

"Jordan, are you okay?" Teresa asked with concern in her eyes.

I wiped my tears with the back of my hand. "Yes."

I wanted to stop crying, but I couldn't. The tears kept falling. I was not in control of my emotions. It was like something was taking over my body. I wanted it to stop, but I had no control.

As the tears continue to fall, I was still able to hear what Pastor Mathews was saying.

"You are all here for a reason. God brought you here and He wants you to leave your troubled past behind. So if you have been through something and you have been holding on to the guilt, the hurt, the bad memories, it's time to let it go and give it all to the Lord. You can't do it alone. Let Him handle it. The battle is not yours it's the Lord. Come now and leave it at the altar."

The battle is not yours it's the Lord, kept playing in my head like a broken record.

Was God speaking to me through Pastor Mathews? I needed to go to the altar, I wanted to go to the altar, but my legs wouldn't move.

Then I heard my mom's voice in my ear saying, "The Devil is a liar." My thoughts were driving me crazy again.

I wanted to tell my thoughts to stop making me crazy, but then, as if Teresa knew

I was fighting with myself, she took my hand and said, "I can go up there with you."

All I could do was look at her with tear filled eyes. I shook my head no because I couldn't open my mouth to speak.

"You don't have to say anything. Let's just go up to the altar so that they can pray for the both of us." Her words were gentle.

"Something really bad happened to me and I need to tell someone so that God will forgive me," I blurted out without even knowing that I was saying it. I covered my mouth with my hand. If Teresa knew what happened to me she would probably think that I was a bad person. "Never mind, I don't know what I'm saying," I stumbled over my words, trying to clean up the mess I was in.

"Jordan, can you walk up there with me, I need prayer."

"Okay." I inhaled then exhaled, hoping that would give my legs the strength to hold my body while I walked to the altar.

As Pastor Mathews held both Teresa's and my hand, he prayed for wisdom, strength, guidance, courage and forgiveness. I was crying a river. I guess the Pastor knew that something was wrong with me because next thing I knew, I was in a small room sitting at a table with Pastor

Mathews, a Pastor with a thick mustache, and my camp counselor.

"Jordan, I just want to tell you that there is no pain that Jesus can't heal and no hurt that he can't feel," Pastor Mathews said as he held my sweaty hands.

The other pastor gave me a Kleenex to clean my face. He gave me another after seeing that one just wouldn't do. They sat in silence as I released my sorrow and tears in to the Kleenex. My head throbbed so bad that I wanted to just lie down on the table.

"Who hurt you, Jordan?" Pastor Mathews asked softy.

My eyes shot wide open like saucers. They could tell that I'd been hurt. Then I thought for a second. *Duh, I wouldn't be crying if I wasn't hurt.*

I stayed silent.

"We want to help you," the Pastor with the thick mustache said. He stood beside me and then put his hand on my back. I jumped forward. He noticed that I was uncomfortable.

"I'm sorry," his voice was gentle.

I was so tired of holding on to the secret. I was so tired of crying. I was so tired of my thoughts taking over my emotions. I was so tired of walking around acting like everything was okay. I was so tired of being tired.

I had come to grips at that very moment and realized that I needed to speak out. Not just for me, but for the other girls that never spoke out. But I knew I wasn't releasing this secret by myself, I was not alone. The message that Pastor preached kept coming back to me. The battle is not yours it's the Lord.

I held my head low. My legs shook under the table.

"I... was ...raped... by my mother's boyfriend," I cried out. I'd finally built up enough courage to say it out loud to someone.

I had no clue what was going to happened next, but at that very moment a heavy weight was lifted from me.

Chapter 13

The car ride home was long as I wondered what my mom was thinking. Pastor Mathews called my mother and told her what I had confessed to him and the other Pastor. Was she angry with me? Had she told Darnell? Would I have to face the both of them when I got home? I was not ready to face them. My mother had called my phone, but I didn't answer. I didn't know what to say to her.

Before I left the camp grounds, Pastor Mathews prayed with me and told me that if I needed anything or just needed to talk I could call or email him. My counselor told me the same thing.

I was glad I told because I didn't think I could live my life keeping that secret any longer. My hurt was still full of pain because it happened, but one day I knew I would be able to help someone just like Pastor Mathew said I would.

My phone rang and it brought me back to reality. It was a text from my mom. My heart raced and my palms shook as I pushed the button to see what she text me.

Jordan, he is no longer here. Nanna and I are here waiting on you. I love you.

I exhaled. *Does that mean she's not mad at me?* I didn't text back. I just sat back in my seat and waited until the car pulled into my drive way.

My mother stood on the porch as I got my suitcase out of the truck and waved bye to Teresa and her parents. As I walked towards my mother I saw her face was filled with sorrow like someone had died. She hugged me and I hugged her back.

My heart beat at an irregular pace. I didn't know what hit me, but I just ran in the house and up the steps to my bedroom, not even speaking to my grandmother who was sitting on the couch, right by the spot where I was violated.

I sat on my bed with my face buried in my hands. Was I ever going to stop crying? My mother entered the room and stood in the doorway.

"Jordan, talk to me." She whispered like she was out of breath, not trying to comfort me. She acted as if I was a fungus and she didn't want to come close to me.

"What do you want me to say?" I wailed. I was angry.

"Darnell treated you as if you were his daughter. Tell me that Darnell didn't …touch you." Her face grew haggard with worry.

Then I looked in her eyes. It was like she was begging me with her eyes to tell her it was not true.

When she said his name I grew full of rage and I didn't know where it came from. I stood up and walked up to her. Was she believing him over me?

"Well, Mom, he did more than touch me, he raped me," I cried out.

My mom stared into my eyes like she wanted to say something. A tear dropped from her right eye and then she turned around and walked out of my room. I just stood there. I didn't move, I watched her from behind until I couldn't see her any more. Then I suddenly heard a loud thump.

I walked slowly out of my room to see what it was. I didn't have the energy to run, I was emotionally drained again. I saw my mother on the ground at the end of the stairs, my grandmother by her side.

"Jasmine," my grandmother called out.

"Mom, are you okay?" My stomach was suddenly in knots.

"Yes, I just got a little weak, but I'll be alright," she mumbled with tears in her eyes as she stood to her feet. Then she continued, "Let's go, Jordan. We're going to the ER to get you checked out and to make a police report."

My mom limped over to get her purse and she walked out of the front door with my grandmother's help.

I followed quietly behind them.

I told the doctor that the sexual abuse happened over three weeks ago. They still did an exam even though they didn't think they would find anything because it was so long ago. They tested me for STD's and gave me pills to kill any sexually transmitted diseases that he may have given to me.

I had to tell my story to the doctor, the sexual abuse victim's advocate, and to the police officer to make a report. They would not allow my mother or grandmother in the room while they questioned me. After about two hours, they released me and they told my mom that a detective that dealt with the sexual abuse of minors would be contacting us soon so he could speak to me. Also, they told my mom that she had to call and make me an appointment with the Family and Child Abuse Prevention Center so I could start counseling sessions.

Everyone kept telling me I was very brave for not keeping it a secret. They also told me that most victims didn't tell, or if they did tell, it was years later. They were very supportive and they believed me, which made me feel like a survivor.

My mother and grandmother even told me that they were proud of me for telling even though it took me three weeks. My mom told me that I didn't ever have to worry about seeing Darnell again.

When we got home, I was getting ready for bed. My mom must have thought I was still in the shower, I heard her crying. Her door was ajar so I peek into her room. I saw her praying, she was on her knees and her body was slouched across the bed. I listen to her as she prayed out loud.

"Lord, why did something so horrifying have to happen to my daughter." She sobbed. "I trusted Darnell I was only trying to help him because I didn't want him to be homeless. Lord I've tried to be the best mother I could be, I've always tried to protect my children from danger. But I let this happened to my daughter I allowed that monster to live under my roof...Uggg." She paused and then continued. "Lord please guide Jordan in the right direction, please give her the strength she needs to pull her through and help her to understand that it was not her fault. Please Lord, heal her mind, body and soul. Please Lord, give me strength and show me how to be there for my child." My mom cried out all her pain in her prayer.

I hated seeing my mom in so much pain; I had never seen her cry before. I tip toed to my room, got on my knees and prayed for strength, guidance and wisdom for my family. I was able to sleep worry free, something I hadn't done in weeks.

Chapter 14

I woke up with a free spirit as I recapped the night before. I was actually proud of myself for confessing and leaving everything at the altar. What if I had not gone to camp? I would still be holding on to that dirty secret.

I realized that God puts us right where we need to be. I never thought that I would have opened up to strangers. The Pastor said that God tests us to see if we can be strong enough to handle bigger things in life. I still wondered why God tested me in the way that he did. *Would there be worst things in my life than this that I would have to conquer?*

My thoughts were ceased when I heard voices downstairs. I walked quietly down the stairs and stopped before I got to the last step to hear the commotion without being seen. My mom and grandmother were talking.

"Mom, I can't believe this happened in my house. I can't believe that Darnell would do anything like this. When I asked him what happened he acted like he didn't know what I was talking about. He said that Jordan was probably making it up because she may have been mad that we had gotten back together," my mom cried out.

Then she continued. "Darnell and I may have argued in the past, but I never in a million years thought that he would have done anything to harm my kids. He treated her like his daughter." Then she paused and I could hear her pacing the hardwood floors.

"What if he planned this all along? He planned to ask me to stay with me to violate my daughter. He had only been staying here for about a month. He wouldn't let her wash dishes, he would fix her plate, and he was always around her. What if he planned this? He planned to be nice to her and he…raped her. He raped my baby. This is all my fault. I trusted him," my mom cried out loud.

I could hear my grandmother trying to comfort her. Silent tears fell from my eyes.

"Jasmine, this is not your fault nor is this Jordan's fault. We all trusted Darnell, but now we see that he is a sick man and—"

"He ain't no man!" My mom spat. "But one thing I do know, his behind is going to jail for what he did. I have tried all of Jordan's life to protect her from something like this. I never allowed her to go over to a friend's house I didn't know. I made sure that wherever she went, I knew what was going on and who would be there. And look at what happened, I couldn't even protect her from a bastard that was living under my roof." She paused.

"What's wrong, Jasmine?" I heard my grandmother ask.

"Oh, my God! What will I tell Justin? One day I will have to tell him that his dad hurt his sister." She paused again. Then she continued. "No, he will never see Darnell again in his life. But then, when he gets older, will Justin be angry at me from keeping him away from his father?"

"Jasmine, don't worry about that now. You have time to think about that stuff later. Now we both need to stay strong for Jordan and Justin. Jordan will get counseling, but you should get some therapy yourself to help you cope with this," my grandmother said.

"I will," my mom said softly.

"But now we have to get Jordan and Justin up because the caseworker from Children Services Bureau will be coming soon to talk to both of them."

"Mom, what if they think that I am an unfit mother for allowing this to go down in my house?" My mom wept.

"Calm down now before the kids hear you. You are a good mom and they will see that you are doing all you can to get your daughter the help she needs and to get Darnell behind bars. They will not take your kids from you," my grandmother assured her.

I had heard enough.

I walked back to my room, got my robe and then went to the bathroom and took a hot shower to release all the tension I had.

"I'm way too young for all this stuff to be clouding my mind," I said to myself.

Chapter 15

My mom and I were in the car on our way to Detective Hunter's office. The visit with the caseworker from CSB went well. She came out, checked out the house and talked to Justin and me. She told my mother to make an appointment for therapy. She believed that I was telling the truth and she closed the case and she went on her merry way.

Detective Hunter was really nice. It was easy to talk to him, he wasn't demanding and he was very caring and patient with me. We talked in a small office with a long rectangle table. Before he asked me any questions, he informed me that he would be recording what I told him.

Why didn't they record me the first time instead of making me repeat my story to different people? I was getting tired of reliving it over and over again.

My mom had to sit in the lobby. When I was done with the detective my mom went into the room to talk to him. When they were done he met with the both of us and said that he would start looking for Darnell so that he could question him. But in the mean time I would have to meet with the Prosecutor that would be handling the case. I would have to appear before a grand jury and the prosecutor would ask me questions in front of them.

"I will be in a room full of people listening to my story?" I asked. Chills ran down my spine.

"Yes, Jordan but you are doing well. You are a very smart girl and there is no need to be scared. Jessica is the prosecutor on your case and she will be right there by your side. I will be there too. So there is no need to worry, you will be fine," he said, trying to lift my spirts.

"Can I go in with her?" My mom asked.

"No, Jessica will be there with her," the detective answered.

I could tell my mom was becoming frustrated because she was not able to be by my side.

I had been attending my counseling sessions, Amanda was very nice. I'm glad I was able to talk t a young counselor and not some old person. The first few days we went over a lot of paper work. Then she gave me a handbook and explained to me what child sexual abuse was and that it could be physical, nonphysical, and exploitive. Then she gave me some examples.

We also talked about the short-term and long term effects of child sexual abuse and rape. She also told me that anger, depression, shame, guilt, and confusion were all feelings associated with sexual abuse. I was glad I wasn't the only person going through all those emotions. I thought I was going crazy.

I learned so much about why people abused others. Darnell was just a sick human being and he needed help. I probably wasn't the only one he'd violated.

She also prepared me so that I would be ready to stand in front of the grand jury.

"I don't think I will be able to talk in front of a lot of people," I told Amanda. My stomach fluttered just thinking about it.

"Jordan, you will do great. The prosecutor will be there and she will make you feel comfortable. You don't even have to look at the people, just look at the prosecutor. She will ask you a few questions and then it will be over. Then the police will be able to find Darnell and put him behind bars. Jordan, you are very strong, you know that?"

"Yeah, thanks."

"Most people don't tell because they have been taught to obey adults even when they are doing wrong. Some are scared to tell the secret because of fear of being hurt by the abuser again. Some have been bribed to keep the secret. Some are ashamed to tell. And some have been convinced that the abuse is normal or okay. But most victims feel guilty because they may believe that the abuse was their fault.

"But you… you are a very strong girl. I'm so proud of you because you didn't hold on to that secret. You told someone. You will do great," she said as she carried a proud look on her face.

I was still nervous. "How many people will be in the room?" I swallowed dryly.

"Um, no more than ten," Amanda replied.

"Will there be men there?" My voice quavered.

"Most likely there will be men in the jury." She got up from her seat and tried to comfort me by placing her hand on my shoulder. "Jordan, don't worry, it is not as bad as you think it is. It will only take about ten to twenty minutes and it will be over." She was precise.

"Will there be a judge there?"

"No, just you, the detective, the prosecutor and the jury," she said with a calm smile.

She could say it wasn't going to be bad because she wasn't walking in my shoes. Different shows on TV flashed in my mind when people were on trial and the victim had to talk in from of a lot of people while they sat next to the judge hitting the wooden hammer.

I was not looking forward to talking in front of a jury.

Chapter 16

Today was the day I would be standing in front of the jury. I was exhausted as my mom drove to the court house. I tossed and turned in bed the night before, I didn't get one wink of sleep. I was so nervous. I had never talked in front of strangers before about something so agonizing.

"Jordan, I'm so proud of you. You are so strong and I'm so blessed to have you as my daughter. I have tried all your life to protect you from everything, I am so sorry I wasn't there to protect you from Darnell." Her voice was shaky as if she wanted to cry.

I swallowed the lump that was in my throat, but I kept quiet.

"I wish I could be there for you while you talk in front of the jury, but I can't. But I will be right outside of the door waiting on you. I can tell that you are nervous, but I know you can do it. The hard part is over, now all you have to do is answer the few questions that Jessica has for you and then it will be all over." She rubbed my leg to comfort me as she drove.

When we pulled up to the court house my legs shook and I could barely walk. I wore a black short sleeved dress with stockings. Detective Hunter and Jessica were there waiting on me. They both told me that I looked nice and it was going to be quick and easy and I wouldn't have to answer any more questions or tell my story over to another stranger.

After my mom said a quick prayer with me, I walked into the room behind Jessica and the detective. There were three black women, two black men, two white men and three white women sitting in chairs. Jessica walked me over to a chair in from of them but not facing them and I sat down.

"What is your full name?" Jessica asked.

"Jordan Colbert." I swallowed the lump in my throat.

"How old are you, Jordan?"

"Fifteen."

"Who is Darnell Davis?"

"My brother's father."

"How long have you known Darnell?"

"For about six years." My hands began to sweat from being nervous.

"What name did he call you?"

"Baby girl," I said and I heard someone gasp in the jury.

"Did Darnell touch you in places that you did not want to be touched?"

I swallow hard. "Yes." Beads of sweat lined my hairline.

"Jordan, please briefly tell me what happened that day when you and Darnell were alone?"

I cleared my throat. I knew this would be the last time I had to tell my story. Even though I didn't want to, I did, to get it over with. My heart pumped spastically. Jasmine nodded her head as if she were saying you can do it.

"I went downstairs to eat my dinner. I didn't know Darnell was there, but he was sitting on the couch in the living room. He shocked me. I had turned around to go back upstairs, but he told me to go and eat my dinner before it got cold." My leg shook as I spoke. I licked my dry lips, then I continued.

"When I was done eating, I walked back through the living room to go up to my room. But that's when Darnell pulled me to the ground, pushed my shorts and panties to the side and put his penis inside me. I don't know how long I was there, but I pushed him off of me and I ran to my room. I didn't want it to happen. I was scared." I exhaled, I was done. I hoped Jessica didn't ask me any more questions.

"Okay, thank you, Jordan. That's all the questions I have for you," Jessica said.

I nodded, got up from my seat and walked out of the room with my head hung low. I exhaled again after I was in the lobby with my mom. I was so relieved that it was over.

Detective Hunter and Jessica told me I was strong and that I was an amazing person. As we drove home from the courthouse, there were a few questions that I needed to ask my mom.

"Mom, is Darnell in jail yet?" I pushed my words out.

"Nope, the police are looking for him now."

"So, he's on the run?" I spat with fear.

"Yup, but don't worry, Jordan, he cannot come near us. I gave Detective Hunter a few addresses where I thought Darnell might be hiding. They will find him soon," she spoke calmly as if she wasn't worried.

I knew that Detective Hunter and my mom had had a few phone conversations and I was really curious about what Darnell had told him when he spoke to him. "Mom, I know you know some of the things that Darnell told the detective…what did he tell him?" I asked.

"Jordan I don't think this is the right time to tell you what Darnell has said."

"But, mom, I want to know," I demanded.

My mom looked at me for a few seconds and then said, "First he tried to deny that anything happened between you and him. But then Detective Hunter lied and said that he had his DNA. Then Darnell told him that you were promiscuous and that you came on to him."

"Promiscuous! He's a liar!" I boomed. I couldn't believe he was telling people I was the reason he raped me. I was livid.

"Jordan, calm down. I know he's a liar and Detective Hunter knows he is a liar. He said your story was strong and you never changed it," Mom said sternly.

No wonder they kept telling me to repeat my story, to see if I would change it. "So why didn't they just arrest him then?"

"Because they didn't have enough evidence. But now that the jury has reached a verdict, they can pick him up."

Then I thought about Justin. His father would be going to jail. He loved his father. How would that affect him?

"I know Justin will be sad if Darnell goes to jail," I pouted.

"Jordan, don't you worry about Justin. I will talk to him when he is old enough to understand. But now it's all about you and your healing process. Darnell needs to be put behind bars for a long time for what he's done to you. I want you to stop worrying because that can cause a lot of stress on you. Okay."

"Okay," I said. I wished it was just that easy to say okay and stop worrying, but it wasn't.

Chapter 17

My mom, Justin, and I had spent the day at the carnival. I had a great time and I know Justin had a ball. A few weeks ago Detective Hunter called my mom and told her that they had Darnell in custody. They found him hiding out in one of his friend Jerry's house, the same friend that Darnell had cutting our grass.

Before Darnell was arrested, I heard my mom talking to my grandmother. She was saying that Jerry told her that Darnell told him that my mom put him out because he was cheating on her. He was definitely a liar and wasn't going to tell his friend the truth.

I stopped having nightmares. On some days I still wondered why me, but I didn't allow my thoughts to drive me crazy. I kept my journal that Amanda told me to write in when I felt like expressing my emotions on paper. I really liked attending counseling, I learned a lot of things about myself and I learned ways to control my anger when I thought about the past.

I also started writing poetry. Maybe one day I will publish a poetry book.

"Jordan, I have some news to tell you," my mom said after she hung up her cell phone. Justin was riding on the motorcycle ride.

"What's up, Mom?" I asked, eating my cotton candy.

"That was Jessica on the phone," she said as she looked me dead in the eyes.

I knew the only reason why the prosecutor would be calling my mom.

"What she say?" I wanted to know.

"Darnell got sentenced to seven years in prison and when he gets out, he will be on the Registered Sex Offenders list for the rest of his life."

I didn't know what to think. I didn't know what to say.

"How do you feel about that?" My mom wanted to know.

"I don't know," I said, because I didn't know what I felt.

The guy that violated me would be locked up for seven years. Yes, he deserved it because he shouldn't have done what he did. But that same guy was my brother's father and my brother would be fatherless for seven years.

One year later…

I am not what has happened to me I am
what I choose to become.
- Jordan Colbert

My sweet sixteen birthday party was right around the corner and I couldn't wait. My mom and dad were throwing me a party at a nice hall. They were going to get me a Deejay, the food would be catered, and I would be able to invite all my friends.

I was so excited. I had to think of a theme, but I just didn't know what theme I wanted. I still had to find me something to wear. I had so much to do and only a little bit of time.

"It's tough being a teenager, so many decisions to make. But I can handle it," I smiled.

Despite of what I had been through over the past year, I was still able to keep my grades up at school. I decided to change what I wanted to major in when I when to college. Instead of becoming a veterinarian, I want to become a Child Psychologist. I wanted to help children that were in need. I wanted to be the voice for those who were scared to speak up for themselves.

My mother and I had become closer than we had ever been before and she even started going to counseling. My little brother was getting big. He still got on my nerves every now and then, but I loved him to death.

I would be getting my car soon. My dad told me that he would buy me one after I got my license. I had my temporary permit to drive and I had been driving with my mom. She was a nervous wreck. She said I was a good driver, yet she acted as if I was going to hit everything in sight. But she also told me I'd better find a job because she wouldn't be paying for gas for my car.

I continued to see my counselor twice a week, it was really helping me to cope with what had happened. If I hadn't gone to counseling I would still be angry, confused, and stuck. I knew I had a long road ahead of me, but I was taking it just one day at a time.

I knew that I was not the only person that had had tragedy in my life and I knew that what happened was not my fault. I knew that I would be just fine as long as I kept my faith in God. I loved my life and I knew that God only put us through tough situations to make us stronger.

As for Darnell, he was a sick man. I trusted him and he violated and deceived me. I had learned to forgive him, but I would never forget what he had done to me. I hoped he got the help that he needed while he was in prison.

People may sometimes wonder why they may be in the abyss that they are in. But if they believe, God will pull them through. He will not put more on them than they can bear.

My heart and soul were wrecked and I wasn't sure if I would make it, but I did. And I learned that sometimes what you're most afraid of doing is the very thing that will set you free.

I AM FREE!

The reasons behind this story…

According to Rape, Abuse & Incest National Network, each year there are about 293,000 victims of sexual assault. (www.rainn.org) The reason I wrote this book was because there are so many people (girls, women, boys and men) that have been sexually abused (molested or raped) as a child/teen and there are only a few that have told someone.

Most of the time the abuser is someone close to the victim, maybe a family member, a teacher, the next door neighbor or a close friend of the family. Most victims do not tell on their abuser because of fear or because they have been threatened, or they're ashamed, or they think it is their fault.

Some don't tell because they think no one will believe them or maybe they think they deserved it. Jordan was scared, but she built up the courage. And with her faith in God, she was able to confess her secret and put her abuser behind bars.

What is child sexual abuse?

It's sexual activity between an adult and a person under the age of eighteen.

Physical abuse is fondling a person or touching them in a sexual way, making a child/teen touch adults or others children/teens' sexual organs, oral contact with genitals involving a child/teen and an adult, and penetration, attempted penetration or any genital-to-genital contact.

Nonphysical abuse is indecent exposure, talking to a child/teen about sex for inappropriate reasons, or telling sexual stories, sending sexually oriented e-mails or text messages to a child/teen, allowing a child/teen to watch or hear sexual acts or materials and showing a child pornography or other inappropriate sexual material.

Exploitive abuse is child pornography, child prostitution, sex rings and internet exploitation

If a child or teen has been sexually abused then there can be a lot of long term effects such as low self-esteem, guilt, shame, feeling of betrayal , depression, anger and difficulty in forming trusting, meaningful relationships.

If you are a teen that has been molested and are reading this book, please tell someone what has happened to you. It's never too late to tell. Just think, what if that person is sexually abusing other people? You may be scared, but if you tell it will lift so much weight off of you.

You may think no one will believe you, but tell a police or a teacher. They have to report it and someone will look in to it. You have a voice, please use it, you will feel much better after you get it off your chest. You will feel so much better because you will have someone to talk to and help you through your pain. You are not the only that this has happened to, so you are not alone. It's not your fault. You didn't deserve it. You are a survivor.

If you are a parent and you are reading this book, your child may have been sexually abused and you may be shocked, overwhelmed with guilt, anger, disgusted, or you may feel like you are a bad parent because you didn't see it coming. Please know that the best thing for you to do is get your child some help.

Get the law enforcement involved. And after that is done, be open-minded with your child, be very supportive and be willing to listen to your child when they need to talk, but don't pry.

This was a tough topic for me to speak on. But there are a lot of Jordan's in the world Today, girls and boys who are filled with so many emotions and scared to turn their abuser in. Some are confused about what they should and shouldn't do because of the pain they may think they will cause in their family.

I felt that it was important to write this story because I wanted to be the voice for the voiceless and I'm trying to illuminate topics that some people are trying so hard to keep in the dark. I hope this book has helped someone that thought that they would never tell on their abuser for whatever reasons.

I hope that Jordan gave you the courage to speak your truth.

For more information about sexual assault, or to find a local counseling center, or for an online hotline, or statistics, go to this website. www.rainn.org.

This is episode two of three stories in my Teenage Sorrow Series. Book one is Heaven's Cry. Please leave a review on Amazon.com and tell me your thoughts.

Check out www.charmainegalloway.com for my other titles. I appreciate you for giving my work a chance. Be on the lookout for My Sister's Keeper: Tera and LaToya's Story, part three of this series.

Blessings

Charmaine Galloway

About the Author

Charmaine Galloway was born and currently resides in Toledo, Ohio with her two children. Writing has been her passion and a positive emotional outlet since middle school. As a teen, writing in her journal allowed her to escape from the negativity of her world. Around that time she also began writing her debut poetry book.

Charmaine has a Bachelor of Arts in Family Life Education and an Associate's Degree in Early Childhood Education. Titles by Charmaine includes: My World, Through My Eyes, Girlfriends Secrets, The Secrets They Kept, Tyree's Love Triangle, Golden, Heaven's Cry, Girl Talk, Find The Princess Within, Mommy's Little Superhero and I Love Myself As I Am.

Ms. Galloway is passionate about writing reality based stories about imperfect people. She hopes to enlighten, inspire, and touch the hearts of her readers. She is currently working on new projects, so keep a look out for her upcoming releases.

Charmaine Galloway